Blossom
the Flower Girl
Fairy

For Emmett and Theo

Special thanks to AnnMarie Anderson

All rights reserved. Published by Scholastic Inc., *Publishers since 1920.* SCHOLASTIC and associated logos are trademarks and/or registered trademarks of Scholastic Inc. RAINBOW MAGIC is a trademark of Rainbow Magic Limited. Reg. U.S. Patent & Trademark Office and other countries. HIT and the HIT logo are trademarks of HIT Entertainment Limited.

The publisher does not have any control over and does not assume any responsibility for author or third-party websites or their content.

ISBN 978-0-545-85202-9

10 9 8 7 6 5 4 3 2 1   16 17 18 19 20

Printed in the U.S.A.   40

First edition, February 2016

Blossom
the Flower Girl
Fairy

by Daisy Meadows

SCHOLASTIC INC.

The Fairyland Palace

Rachel's House

Bedroom

Garden

Tippington Town

Weddings, flower girls, cakes galore,
Royal weddings are such a bore.
I'll do my best to spoil this one,
Those fairies won't have any fun!

When I steal Blossom's magic things,
Say good-bye to vows and rings.
No one will get married today,
If Jack Frost has his frosty way!

**Find the hidden letters in the stars throughout
this book. Unscramble all 7 letters to spell a
special wedding word!**

A Tisket,
A Tasket

Contents

A Fairy Godmother

"Isn't it the most beautiful dress you've ever seen?" Rachel Walker said with a sigh as she tucked a blond curl behind her ear.

Her best friend, Kirsty Tate, nodded dreamily. "Oh, it is!" she exclaimed.

The dress was a magnificent white wedding gown covered in sparkling

rhinestones and delicate lace. Rachel's aunt Angela held it in front of her as she twirled around playfully.

"You look just like a princess!" Rachel told her aunt.

Aunt Angela laughed. "I'm no princess," she told her niece. "I'm more of a fairy godmother. I make dreams come true!"

That was the truth. Aunt Angela was a wedding planner. It was her job to organize weddings down to the tiniest detail, and she was

very good at it. Her company, Fairy
Tale Weddings, was incredibly successful.

Rachel and Kirsty exchanged a smile
at the mention of fairy godmothers.
The two friends knew a lot about
fairies. They had first met fairies while
vacationing on Rainspell Island. Now
they had many fairy friends and had
visited Fairyland lots of times. Jack Frost
and his mischievous goblins caused a lot
of problems
there, and
Rachel
and Kirsty
were the fairies'
secret helpers.

In fact, that's
what the girls
were doing

today—being helpful! Aunt Angela had hired them to be her wedding planning assistants. Today they were at the hotel where the wedding party was staying, in case Aunt Angela needed two extra pairs of hands.

The next day's wedding was to be Tippington's largest of the year. The wedding was so big there were going to be six flower girls. Rachel and Kirsty weren't as experienced as Aunt Angela, but the girls had been bridesmaids in Kirsty's cousin Esther's wedding, so they knew a thing or two about brides and bouquets.

"This wedding is going to be amazing, Aunt Angela," Rachel said happily. "I just know it!"

"Thank you, dear," Aunt Angela replied as she gently hung up the bride's gown. Then she ran her hand over the other dresses and suits on the clothes rack. "The clothing is all ready for tomorrow. But I really should go over the flower order. Then I need to talk with the caterer about the food, call the party rental company, double-check that the band will be there on time, and confirm the address for the photographer."

"Whoa!" Kirsty murmured, her eyes wide. "It sounds like you have a lot to do. We're happy to help."

"That would be great," Aunt Angela agreed. She opened a thick blue binder and read over a few pages thoughtfully. Finally, she removed a sheet of paper.

"First, let's focus on the flowers," she said. "Here's the receipt."

She studied it closely, her brow furrowed in concentration.

"Wait a minute," she mumbled as she looked at the paper more closely. "There's something wrong."

"Oh no!" Rachel cried. "What is it?"

"Well, there are six flower girls," Aunt Angela explained. "There's Talia and Tamara—they're twins. Then there's Ashlyn and Avery. They aren't twins, but they are sisters. And finally, there's Mila and Sasha. That means there should be six baskets of rose petals on the order form, but I only see five. I'd better call the flower shop right away."

Rachel and Kirsty waited anxiously while Aunt Angela made the call. But a moment later, she hung up the phone without saying a word with a puzzled look on her face.

"There was no answer," she told the girls. "But I'm certain the flower shop is open today. I'm afraid I don't have time to go there myself, but maybe you girls can?"

"Of course!" Rachel said.

"Yes, we'd be happy to," Kirsty agreed.

"Thanks so much!" Aunt Angela replied as she gave Rachel a quick peck on the cheek. "I knew there was a reason I hired you girls!"

Rachel and Kirsty headed outside. The flower shop was just a few blocks away from the hotel, so it was an easy walk.

"I wonder why no one answered the phone," Kirsty mused. "That seems odd, especially when they have such a big wedding coming up tomorrow."

Rachel just shrugged. "Maybe that's exactly why no one answered," she said. "Everyone at the shop must be busy getting ready for the wedding!"

But when the girls got to Fabulous Flowers, the store was dark inside. Kirsty tugged on the door handle, but it didn't budge. Rachel noticed a sign was posted on the door with the store's hours.

"That's strange," she said. "According to this, the store should definitely be open now."

Kirsty and Rachel weren't sure what to do next. If the flower shop was closed,

how would the flowers be ready in time for the wedding the next day?

"What should we do now?" Kirsty wondered aloud.

"I don't know," Rachel replied. "If there are no flowers tomorrow, the wedding will be ruined!"

The Missing Basket

The girls stood in front of the flower shop, trying to figure out what to do next. Then Kirsty noticed something moving inside the shop.

"Hey!" she said, nudging Rachel. "Look! Someone's inside."

The girls pressed their faces against the windowpane. Sure enough, there was a

figure sitting in the shop in the dark.
From her long hair, it looked to be a
young woman. But she didn't look
happy. She was hunched over, and her
shoulders were shaking.

Kirsty
and Rachel
knocked gently
on the door.
The girl inside
looked up
suddenly,
wiping her
eyes. Then she
came to the door and unlocked it,
pulling the door open.

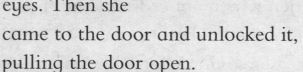

"Can I help you?" she asked Rachel
and Kirsty. The girls noticed that her
eyes were red and rimmed with tears.

"I hope so," Rachel said softly. "But is the shop open?" She pointed to the sign in the store window.

"And are you okay?" Kirsty added, looking genuinely worried. The poor girl seemed very upset.

The girl seemed confused for a moment, and then her face grew pale.

"Oh my goodness!" she cried. "I didn't realize it was time to open the shop. I've been so distracted and upset all morning. Please come in."

The girls stepped inside as the sales girl hurried to turn on the lights. Then she

grabbed a green apron with flowers stitched on it and tied it on over her clothes.

"Please forgive me," she said. "What can I do for you?"

"We have a question about the flower order for tomorrow's wedding," Rachel said.

But at the word *wedding*, the girl burst into tears again!

Rachel and Kirsty glanced at each other, unsure of what to do.

"Can you tell us what's wrong?" Kirsty asked gently. "Maybe we can help. We're good problem solvers."

"That's very kind of you," the girl replied with a sigh. "But I don't think you can help me. Today's my birthday, and my fiancé and I had a big fight this morning. He came over this morning to drive me to work and give me my birthday present. But it was the worst gift ever! He gave me a baseball glove and baseball tickets, but I hate baseball! I was so surprised, I burst into tears. And now I'm getting cold feet about our wedding! How can I marry someone who doesn't understand me at all? I'm not going to be able to get any work done today."

"Wow," Kirsty replied. "That's a tough one."

Rachel nodded sympathetically. Then she noticed a sparkle in the flowerpot on the counter behind the sales clerk. The pink peonies seemed to be glowing!

At that moment, the phone rang, and the girl excused herself. She headed to the back of the shop to answer the call.

"Oh, Kirsty, look!" Rachel said, pointing to the flowerpot just as a tiny fairy with gossamer wings peeked her head out of the basket.

"Hello," she said sweetly. "I'm Blossom the Flower Girl Fairy."

Rachel and Kirsty gasped in delight.

Blossom had brown skin and curly hair piled into a bun on top of her head. She wore a crown of flowers and leaves wound around her curls. Her pink taffeta dress was decorated with pink peonies and lace, and she wore  a beautiful corsage on her wrist. She was lovely.

Rachel and Kirsty loved meeting new fairies.

"Hello!" Rachel said brightly. "I'm Rachel, and this is Kirsty."

The fairy smiled at the girls, but her mouth quickly turned into a tiny frown and her wings drooped.

"Nice to meet you both," she said. "I'm afraid I need your help. There's a royal wedding tomorrow, but Jack Frost's goblins stole my basket of rose petals. If I don't get it back soon, both the royal wedding *and* your wedding will be ruined!"

"Oh no!" Kirsty said with a gasp.

"That's terrible," Rachel agreed.

"I know," Blossom replied. "My magic protects all flower girls. It's my job to work with Mia the Bridesmaid Fairy to make sure all weddings are happy and magical. But I can't do that without my

magic items! My basket of rose petals
helps prevent misunderstandings between
couples."

Rachel and Kirsty glanced at each
other. They seemed to be having the
same thought.

"That must be why the sales clerk had
that argument with her fiancé!" Kirsty

exclaimed. "It's because Blossom's enchanted basket is missing!"

"That's just what I was thinking," Rachel agreed.

The girls turned back to Blossom. "How can we help?" Kirsty asked.

Blossom fluttered her wings hopefully.

"We've got to get to Fairyland as quickly as possible," she told them. "Will you come?"

"Of course!" Rachel agreed.

Kirsty nodded her head as well.

"Here we go!" Blossom said, pointing her wand at the girls. A second later, a burst of tiny sparkling flowers and

butterflies shot out from the tip of the
wand. They swirled around Kirsty and
Rachel, and the girls quickly shrunk
down to fairy-size, complete with silvery
wings on their backs.

Rachel and
Kirsty fluttered
their wings
happily. No
matter how
many times
they became
fairies, they still
loved it! The girls flew after Blossom,
heading straight for Fairyland.

Into the Woods

They landed in front of a toadstool cottage with a pretty garden out front. A grove of pine trees surrounded the house.

"This is where I live," Blossom explained. "I usually keep my magic items at the Wedding Workshop along with Mia the Bridesmaid Fairy's magic items. But I brought all of my items

home to my cottage to prepare for the royal wedding tomorrow. Queen Titania's niece Princess Rosalyn is marrying Prince Arlo. Mia and I have been preparing for weeks. I'm sure Jack Frost told his goblins to take my basket. They love spoiling parties, and the royal wedding is the biggest party of the year!"

"Are all three of your items missing?" Rachel asked with a look of concern.

"No, just the basket is gone," Blossom replied, looking relieved.

"I'm wearing my other two items to keep them safe."

She pointed to a ribbon tied around her wrist. It sparkled with magic.

"This is my ivory ribbon," Blossom explained. "It controls harmony and makes weddings run smoothly. And my flower crown helps love stay strong in good times and bad."

The fairy reached up to touch the crown of flowers and leaves on her head. It glittered brightly as well.

"Where do you think the basket is now?" Kirsty asked. "Do you

have any idea where Jack Frost or his goblins would have taken it?"

Blossom shook her head sadly.

Rachel and Kirsty looked around the cottage and the surrounding area. They had to find that basket. But it could be anywhere in Fairyland! They had no idea where to begin. Then something caught Rachel's eye.

"Oh, look!" she cried out, pointing across the cottage lawn. A trail of lilac-colored rose petals led into the tall pine trees that surrounded the little house. "Do you think those petals fell out of your basket?"

The three girls fluttered over to the petals.

"You're right!" Blossom cried happily. "Those are from my basket. Purple is the

color of royalty, so I was planning to
sprinkle those petals over the flower girls
at the royal wedding tomorrow."

"Maybe we can follow this trail of
flower petals to find the basket," Kirsty
suggested.

"That's a great idea!" Blossom said.
"There's a path that leads through the
woods to Jack Frost's Ice Castle. I'll bet

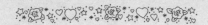

that's where the thieves are taking the basket. If we hurry, maybe we can catch up to them before they get there!"

The three girls flew in the direction of the petals. Sure enough, the trail led down a path through the woods. They had been fluttering along for a few minutes when Rachel heard a rustling in the trees ahead.

"Shhhh!" Rachel whispered, her finger to her lips. "Do you hear that?"

Kirsty nodded. It sounded like voices just ahead of them.

"Let's hide!" Blossom said. "If it's Jack Frost or his goblins, we don't want them to see us right away. It will be better if we can surprise them."

They ducked behind a thick tree trunk that was surrounded by some lush flowering plants and hoped they were well hidden. Then they peeked out to see who was there.

Two goblins with green skin, pointy ears, and long noses stood in a clearing between two trees. They seemed to be arguing over something.

"Look, goblins!" Rachel whispered.

Kirsty noticed that one of the goblins held a white wicker basket. "Is that yours?" she asked Blossom in a hushed tone.

"It is!" Blossom replied softly. "This is definitely the path that leads to Jack Frost's Ice Castle. I'm sure now that's where they're taking it. We have to get it back!"

Kirsty and Rachel were quiet for a minute.

"I wonder what they're arguing about," Rachel mused. "Maybe if we knew, we could figure out how to get the basket back."

The three girls inched closer, being careful to remain hidden in the trees.

Suddenly the goblin on the right grabbed the basket out of the other

30

goblin's hands. He turned the basket
upside down and shook it angrily. All
of the rose petals had fallen out, and the
basket was empty.

"Look what you've done!" he yelled
loudly enough for the girls to hear him
clearly. "You've dropped all the rose
petals!"

"Who cares!" the first goblin shouted back. "Jack Frost only needs the basket to spoil the royal wedding."

"How do you know that?" the other goblin replied. "He told us to grab the basket with the rose petals in it. Maybe he needs the flowers, too. You heard him—if we mess this up, we won't get any dessert ever again!"

The first goblin paled. "Oh no," he moaned. "Anything but that! Bogmallows are my favorite food!"

Blossom motioned to the girls to move a little closer to her.

"Is it true?" Kirsty asked her. "Are the rose petals magical, too, or is it just the basket?"

"It's just the basket," Blossom replied. "The rose petals aren't important."

That gave Rachel a great idea.

"We can use that information to get the basket back!" she exclaimed. "I have a plan. Blossom, can you use your magic to make Kirsty and I look like goblins?"

The fairy smiled and nodded.

"I can," she agreed, "but the magic won't last long. You'll have to work quickly. Can you do that?"

Rachel nodded. Then she leaned in and whispered her idea to Blossom and Kirsty.

Kirsty giggled. It was a silly plan, but with a bit of fairy magic, it just might work.

Goblin Girls

Blossom waved her wand at the girls. Glittering butterflies and flowers swirled around the two friends. First, Kirsty and Rachel grew from fairy-size to goblin-size. Then their wings grew smaller and smaller until they disappeared, while their ears grew taller and pointer, their

noses grew longer, and their skin turned
goblin green.

"Ta-da!" Blossom cried. "Two goblins,
ready to go."

Kirsty stifled a giggle as she looked at
her friend.

"You look pretty funny," she told
Rachel.

"So do you!"
Rachel agreed. "But
I definitely like
being a fairy better
than being a goblin."

"Me, too," Kirsty
agreed. "Let's hurry
and do this so we
can get back to
being fairies as
quickly as we can!"

The girls emerged from the trees and went right over to the goblins.

"Is that for Jack Frost?" Kirsty asked confidently as she pointed to the basket.

"Yes, why?" the goblin holding the basket replied. "And who are you?"

"Jack Frost sent us to find you," Rachel chimed in. "He was wondering what was taking you so long. He needs that basket right away!"

The first goblin got a worried look on his face. "Oh no," he muttered.

"You'd better take that basket straight to him," Rachel ordered sternly. "Otherwise he'll be very unhappy."

She gestured to the basket and pretended to notice for the first time that the rose petals were missing.

"But where are the rose petals?" she asked, faking surprise. "They're supposed to be in there, too! Jack Frost won't want an empty basket."

Kirsty nodded in agreement and crossed her arms, trying her best to look stern. She glanced down at her arms. Oh no! The green color was beginning to fade. She glanced at Rachel. Her friend's

disguise was wearing off, too. Rachel's
ears were slowly shrinking back to their
usual size. Her nose was smaller than it
had been, too. And Rachel herself was
slowly changing back to fairy-size. Kirsty
raised her eyebrows at Rachel.

"We have to hurry!"
Kirsty mouthed to
her friend.

Luckily for the
girls, the goblins were
too busy yelling at
each other to notice
their dissolving disguises.

"See!" shouted one
goblin. "I told you we needed to go back
for the flowers!"

"How was I supposed to know that?"
grumbled the other.

"Why don't we help you out?" Rachel said smoothly. "We'll take the basket straight to Jack Frost, and you two can go back for the rose petals."

"But I want the credit for stealing the basket!" the first goblin whined. "If you take it to him, he won't let me borrow his wand like he promised."

Kirsty glanced at Rachel. Her disguise had faded even more, and Rachel was even smaller. What were they going to do? They had to get the basket from the goblins—and fast!

"Uh, but you're already in trouble with Jack Frost," Kirsty

reminded them, thinking quickly. "I doubt he'll let you borrow his wand now, anyway. So you may as well go get the rose petals while we take the basket to him right away."

The goblins hesitated for a moment, and Rachel took advantage of their indecision. She stepped forward and reached out, grabbing the basket. A moment later, Blossom darted out from the trees. Rachel quickly passed the basket to her, and it shrunk back to fairy-size.

"Thanks!" Blossom said cheerfully as the girls' disguises dissolved completely, leaving them looking like their fairy-sized selves again.

"Hey!" The first goblin scowled. "No fair! You're fairies, not goblins. You tricked us."

"Yeah," whined the other goblin. "That was our basket. Now we're not getting dessert for sure!"

"Sorry, goblins!" Kirsty cried. "But that's what you get for taking something that doesn't belong to you."

Then she, Rachel, and Blossom hurried out of the woods, the goblins chasing after them.

"Give us back that basket!" they screeched. "You'll be sorry, you tricky fairies!"

Blossom and the girls fluttered up
into the sky and back to the cottage,
leaving the goblins far behind them.

"Thank you so much!" Blossom said
happily once they were back at the
cottage. "Now that I have my basket
back, the royal wedding should go off
without a hitch."

At the mention of the royal wedding,
Rachel and Kirsty exchanged a glance.

Both girls had remembered that they had an important job to do, too. They had to get back to Fabulous Flowers to order the extra flower girl basket. If they didn't, Tippington's biggest wedding of the year might be the one that didn't go as planned.

"We've got to get back to the flower shop in Tippington right away," Rachel told Blossom.

"Well, now that you've helped me, let me know if you need *my* help," Blossom told them.

"We might," Kirsty said thoughtfully. "But hopefully the sales clerk and her fiancé have cleared up their misunderstanding now that you have your basket back."

"There's only one way to find out," Rachel said. "We'd better head back to make sure. Bye, Blossom!"

"See you soon, girls," the fairy replied. "And good luck!"

Fabulous Flowers

Rachel and Kirsty entered Fabulous Flowers for the second time that day. This time the lights were on and the door was open. A chime rang as they entered the store, and the sales clerk emerged from the back room, wiping her hands on her apron. She had a big smile on her face.

"Welcome to Fabulous Flowers," she said cheerfully. "Can I help—oh! It's you two again. I was wondering where you went. I thought you had vanished into thin air!"

Kirsty and Rachel giggled. It's true that they had left for Fairyland rather abruptly, and without saying good-bye. But it would have been even stranger to try to explain where they were going. In fact, other humans couldn't know about Fairyland or it would really cause trouble for the fairies.

"Sorry," Rachel said simply. "We forgot we

had something very important to do.
But we're back to talk to you about the
flower order for tomorrow's wedding."

"Of course," the girl replied. "I'm
Allison, by the way. I'm sorry I was
so distraught before. It was very
unprofessional of me."

"That's okay," Kirsty said
sympathetically. "Is everything
okay now?"

"It is!" Allison exclaimed happily. "After
you left, my fiancé came back. He felt
badly because I was so upset, and he
explained everything. He bought me that
baseball glove because I told him a long
time ago that no one had ever taught me
to play. That's why I don't like baseball.
He remembered, and he got me the glove
because he wants to teach me. Then

we'll be able to play catch together at the park."

"How romantic!" Rachel said.

"I know," Allison replied, her cheeks turning red. "I'm embarrassed now that I misunderstood him. It was actually a really thoughtful gift. And remember the baseball tickets I mentioned? They're for opening day. My favorite singer, Hailey

Quick, is singing the national anthem.
Then there's going to be a huge
fireworks show after the game!"

"Wow," Kirsty said. "I love Hailey
Quick. She's awesome. That really is a
cool birthday gift."

"I know," Allison replied. "He's a great
guy. Now what can I do for you? Did
you say something about the flowers for
the wedding at the Botanical Garden
tomorrow?"

"Yes!" Rachel replied. "My aunt is
Angela from Fairytale Weddings. She's
the wedding planner. She thought she
ordered six flower girl baskets, but when
she double-checked the order form, she
only saw five listed. Can you be sure
there are six baskets of rose petals for the
flower girls?"

"Of course!" Allison replied, jotting it down on a piece of paper. "I'll add it to the order right now."

"Thanks," Kirsty replied. She smiled at Rachel. It looked like all of the wedding details were falling back into place now that Blossom had her basket back.

"Now I'd better get back to work," Allison said. "I have a lot to do if I'm going to get all of the flower arrangements done by tomorrow. But don't worry—they're going to be perfect. You'll see!"

Picture
Perfect

Contents

Late for a Date

The next morning, Kirsty was snuggled in her sleeping bag on the floor of Rachel's room, sound asleep. Suddenly, her friend's shout woke her with a start.

"Kirsty, wake up!" Rachel cried. "We overslept! We're going to be late for the photo shoot."

"Oh no," Kirsty replied with a sleepy groan. "What time is it?"

Rachel looked at her fairy alarm clock. Instead of clock hands, two wings pointed at the numbers to tell the time. "It's 9:00, and we're supposed to be there in fifteen minutes! If we hurry, we might

just be a few minutes late."

The girls quickly got dressed, combed their hair, and brushed their teeth. Then they dashed through the kitchen.

"Hi, Mr. Walker!" Kirsty said as she grabbed two bananas from the bowl of fruit on the counter.

Rachel's dad stood at the stove, a spatula in hand as he poured batter onto a hot griddle.

"Whoa!" he replied. "What's the rush? I was just making some of my world-famous chocolate chip pancakes for breakfast."

"Sorry, Dad," Rachel said apologetically. She wished they could stay for breakfast.

Her dad's pancakes really were amazing. "We're late to meet Aunt Angela at the Botanical Garden. We're helping out at the wedding today, remember?"

"Of course!" he replied. "Your mom will give you girls a ride if you promise to at least take some yogurt to eat in the car with those bananas."

"It's a deal!" Rachel said. "Thanks, Dad."

About ten minutes later, the girls hurried through the Botanical Garden entrance gate. A guard pointed the way to the Japanese garden, which is where the photo shoot was taking place.

Aunt Angela was waiting for them underneath a green and red pagoda.

"There you are, girls!" she said with a smile.

"I'm so sorry we're late!" Kirsty burst out. "We overslept."

"It's okay," Aunt Angela said. "The photographer seems to be running behind schedule as well. The bride and groom and the other adults are all still getting ready, but we planned to take pictures of the flower girls first, before they get their dresses dirty. I need to make a few phone calls to see what time he'll be here. Can you girls manage the flower girls until I get back?"

Aunt Angela gestured toward a group of girls in pretty pale-yellow dresses. The smallest two were the same height and had matching headbands. In fact, they were identical twins.

"This is Talia and her twin sister Tamara," Aunt Angela said.

"We're three!" one twin exclaimed, proudly holding up three fingers. The other twin was sucking her thumb and looking very nervous. She took one look at Kirsty and Rachel and burst into tears.

Kirsty stooped down to the girls' level.

"I'm Kirsty," she said. "And this is my friend, Rachel. It's very nice to meet you. We're going to have a lot of fun today, I promise."

Aunt Angela introduced the rest of the girls. There were sisters Ashlyn and

Avery, who were five and nine years old, and cousins Mila and Sasha, who were both six.

"Will you and Kirsty be okay?" Aunt Angela asked Rachel, looking worried for a moment.

"Sure!" Rachel replied confidently. "We have plenty of babysitting experience. It will be fine."

"I've got an idea!" Kirsty said to the girls. She wanted to show Aunt Angela that Rachel was right. They could handle the flower girls—no problem. "Let's play I Spy. We'll all look for things that are a certain color."

"See?" Rachel told her aunt. "Plenty of experience."

Aunt Angela waved good-bye and headed back toward the entrance to the gardens, her cell phone already at her ear.

"I love that game!" exclaimed Mila. "I'll go first. I spy with my little eye something blue."

"That flower is blue," Ashlyn guessed.

"Nope," Mila replied.

"Kirsty's T-shirt?" Rachel guessed.

Mila shook her head.

"The sky!" Ashlyn shouted.

"Yes, that's it!" Mila exclaimed, a smile on her face.

As the girls continued the game, Kirsty felt a tug on her jeans. She looked down to see Talia (or maybe it was Tamara . . . she wasn't exactly sure) looking up at her with wide eyes. She was hopping from one foot to the other.

"Is everything okay?" Kirsty asked. But the little girl didn't reply. She burst

into tears. Then she hopped back and forth a little bit faster.

"Uh-oh!" her twin shouted dramatically. "Talia has to GO! You need to take her to the potty right away!"

Squabbling Sisters

"I've got this," Kirsty said, and she and Talia hurried toward the bathroom immediately. Rachel stayed back with the other girls.

"We're almost there!" Kirsty said encouragingly. "Do you think you can wait just a *tiny* bit longer?"

Talia nodded, but Kirsty noticed that
the little girl walked a bit faster, so Kirsty
quickened her pace, too. She crossed her
fingers and really hoped they made it
in time!

Meanwhile, Rachel was dealing with
her own problems.

"Mom said I could wear the necklace,
and you could wear the
bracelet," Avery told her
sister. "I want the necklace."

"No, she didn't!" Ashlyn
argued. "She said we could
pick, and I picked the
necklace. You take the
bracelet."

The girls were squabbling
over a pretty set of pearls.
Rachel gently touched the

locket she wore around her own neck. It
had been a gift from the fairies, and
it was full of magic fairy dust. If only
Blossom were around right now! She'd
know how to get the sisters to stop
fighting.

"That's not fair,"
Avery whined as
she pulled on the
necklace. "Mom
promised me I
could wear it!"

"Whoa!" Rachel
said, jumping in.
"Let's not pull on it,
girls. It might break,
and then neither of you will be able to
wear it. Why don't you take turns?
Avery can wear it during the photo shoot

and ceremony, and Ashlyn can have it during the reception. Does that work?"

"I guess," Avery said reluctantly.

"That sounds okay," Ashlyn agreed as she gave her sister back the necklace and slipped the bracelet on her own wrist.

"Great," Rachel said, breathing a sigh of relief. Then she caught sight of Kirsty and Talia returning from the bathroom. "You're back!"

"Yup," Kirsty said. "Made it just in time. How are things?"

"They're great," Rachel replied. She was feeling confident again now that Kirsty was back and the sisters had stopped fighting.

back and the sisters had stopped fighting.

"Okay, but bored," Sasha said grumpily. "Hey, look! Can we feed the fish?"

She pointed to a small koi pond nearby. A handful of large orange fish swam around, and there was a dispenser full of fish food pellets near a little wooden bridge that stretched over the pond.

"Sure, I guess so," Rachel replied.

"Just be careful not to get your dresses wet, okay?" Kirsty added.

"Yay!" the girls agreed enthusiastically.

Rachel went over to the dispenser and gathered a handful of the fish food for Talia and Tamara. She gave them a few pellets each and watched as they tossed them gently into the pond and giggled with delight as the fish darted up to eat them.

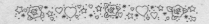

As the older flower girls helped themselves to the fish food, Kirsty gasped. She had just noticed Blossom peeking out from behind the food dispenser. The fairy quickly put her finger to her lips as she ducked out of view. She didn't want the flower girls to see her. It would mean big trouble for the fairies if too many humans knew about Fairyland!

As soon as the younger girls were all busy feeding the fish, Blossom darted over to Kirsty and Rachel. She perched on a low branch of a Japanese maple tree and hid among its leaves.

"How's it going, girls?" Blossom whispered.

"We're doing okay," Rachel replied. "Though we've had one close call and a little fight between sisters."

Blossom looked puzzled. "That's strange," she said. "I was just coming by to let you know that I visited the girls this morning while they were getting ready at the hotel. I sprinkled them with

a little fairy magic to help the day go smoothly for everyone. I even secretly loaned Talia my ivory ribbon. It helps control harmony and order during weddings, which I thought might help you. And I figured it would be farther from Jack Frost in the human world than in the fairy world."

Kirsty and Rachel glanced at the flower girls. All of them were wearing silky ivory ribbons around their waists. That is— all of them except Talia!

"Oh no!" Rachel gasped. "Talia lost the ribbon."

"Or someone snatched it from her!"

74

Blossom groaned. "And I have a pretty good idea who's behind this: Jack Frost! He would love to cause as much chaos as possible at today's royal wedding."

Rachel, Kirsty, and Blossom were so distracted by the missing ribbon that they didn't notice Sasha leaning over the koi pond to get a closer look at the fish. Rachel glanced at the girls just in time to see Sasha's foot slip as she tumbled headfirst into the pond with a giant splash!

Splish, Splash!

A huge gush of water hit Mila and
Ashlyn, who were standing right next
to Sasha.

"Oh yuck!" Sasha moaned as she stood
up in the pond. It wasn't very deep, and
the water only came up to her knees. But
her dress and shoes were completely
soaked.

"I'll help you," Avery said sweetly.
"Here, grab my hand!"

"No, wait!" Rachel shouted as she and
Kirsty rushed over to the pond.

It was too late. Avery had already
leaned over and reached out to the
younger girl, but the ground right around
the pond was muddy and slick. A second
later, there was a second splash as Avery
landed in the pond, too.

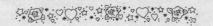

"*Ugh*, icky!" Avery spluttered as she stood up in the water. "Help! The fish are going to bite me!"

Sasha began to cry. "I don't want fish bites!" she sobbed.

Rachel and Kirsty quickly helped both girls out of the muddy water and took a look at everyone. The twins had been spared, but the other four girls were either wet, muddy, or both.

Rachel sighed.

"This would never have happened if Talia was still wearing Blossom's ribbon!" she whispered to Kirsty.

Kirsty nodded, her face serious. "We've got to find it," she agreed gravely.

"What are we going to do?" Avery wailed. "Our dresses are ruined!"

"We'll come up with something, don't

79

worry," Kirsty said. But she sounded
more sure than she felt. She knew they
had to think fast.

"Ouch!" Rachel squeaked, slapping at
her ankle. "I think a mosquito just bit
my leg."

Sasha jumped back and shrieked. "Or a
fish!" she squealed. Avery started yelling
and jumping from one foot to the other.

Kirsty stifled a giggle.

"It's okay, girls," she reassured them. "You're not in the water anymore. Remember?"

Sasha and Avery smiled sheepishly.

Rachel bent down to look at her leg. As she did, Blossom popped out from behind some flowers.

"Oh! It was you!" Rachel whispered. "You startled me."

"Sorry!" Blossom whispered apologetically. "I wanted to get your attention. I tried using my wand to dry the girls' dresses, but my powers are too weak! We have to find the ribbon,

otherwise this
wedding—and the
royal wedding in
Fairyland—will be a
complete disaster."

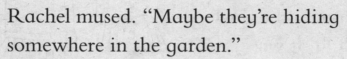

"If the
goblins
took it, they
can't have
gone too far,"
Rachel mused. "Maybe they're hiding
somewhere in the garden."

"You and Kirsty will have to find
the ribbon on your own," Blossom
explained softly. "I can't let the flower
girls see me!"

"Who are you talking to?" Tamara
asked Rachel curiously.

"Oh, no one," Rachel said as she quickly stood up. "I must have been thinking out loud about how much that mosquito bite hurt."

Kirsty had noticed Blossom and Rachel chatting before the fairy darted back to the maple tree to hide from the flower girls. Then Kirsty saw something else—a goblin hiding behind the green and red pagoda! Suddenly, she came up with a plan. She leaned over and quickly whispered her idea to Rachel. Maybe she and

Rachel wouldn't be completely on their own after all.

"That just might work!" Rachel told her friend. Then she turned to the flower girls. "Ready, girls? We're going on a gnome hunt!"

Garden Gnomes Galore

"What's a gnome hunt?" Ashlyn asked.

"Yeah," Sasha chimed in. "And how is that going to fix our dresses?"

"Well," Kirsty began, thinking quickly. "Um, gnomes are creatures that live in gardens—including this one. Sometimes garden gnomes can be very mischievous.

They like to take things that aren't
theirs—like Talia's ribbon!"

Talia looked down and realized that
her ribbon was missing from her dress.
The little girl's eyes went wide, but for
once, she didn't cry. She seemed totally
engrossed in the tale of
the garden gnomes.

"That's right," Rachel
agreed, quickly jumping
in. "But if we can find
the ribbon and get it
back, then everyone's
dresses will magically
be fixed!"

She glanced at Kirsty nervously. Would
the girls go for it? Avery looked a little
skeptical, but the younger girls all seemed
to believe the tall tale.

"Wow!" Sasha said. "Cool. Let's start looking!"

Rachel and Kirsty each took one of the twins, and the other girls spread out across the Japanese garden.

"We're going on a gnome hunt!" Mila sang as she skipped across the little wooden bridge over the koi pond. "Oh! Is that a gnome?"

She pointed at a goblin on the other side of the bridge. The goblin quickly dashed behind a tree.

"Yes!" Rachel shouted. "That's definitely a

gnome: green skin, pointy ears, and a long nose."

Avery's mouth dropped open in disbelief.

"Wow," she said slowly. "They *are* real. Let's go after it!"

The girls raced after the goblin. He darted between the trees and suddenly disappeared.

"Hey, where did it go?" Mila asked. "It was just here a minute ago."

Rachel and Kirsty tried to stay positive.

"Let's keep looking, girls," Rachel said encouragingly.

"This is just like I Spy!" Sasha exclaimed. "And I'm pretty sure I *didn't* spy that fountain earlier."

She pointed to a funny statue in the middle of the koi pond. It was green and goblin-shaped, spitting a fountain of

pond water into the air. And to top it off, there was an ivory-colored ribbon around the statue's waist.

"That's not a fountain, that's a gob—I mean, a garden gnome!" Kirsty shouted, catching herself just in time. For this plan to work, the flower girls had to think the goblins were imaginary garden gnomes, not goblins from Fairyland!

"Catch that gnome!" Mila cried.

The goblin realized he'd been spotted. He froze like a deer caught in a car's headlights. Uncertain of what to do, the goblin grabbed his nose and jumped into the pond.

"Cannonball!" he shouted as he flung himself into the water, splashing the girls on the bank for a second time.

Avery shook herself off but remained focused.

"Rachel?" she asked. "Can gnomes hold their breaths underwater?"

"Um, well, yes," Rachel replied slowly. "But not forever. He'll have to come up for air sometime."

Sure enough, the goblin surfaced a few seconds later, spluttering and spitting out mouthfuls of water. He saw the girls waiting on the bank and quickly swam in the other direction. Then he dashed up and over the bridge. Another goblin poked his head out from behind a tall pine tree. The fountain goblin handed the ribbon to the new goblin. Then he turned and ran back in the opposite direction.

Meanwhile, the goblin with the ribbon climbed up the pine tree. Once he was high enough to be out of reach of the

girls below, he stuck his tongue out
at them.

"Nah-nah-nah-nah-nah," he teased.
"You can't catch me!"

Avery
jumped up
and down,
grabbing for
the ribbon.
But the goblin
was too high.

"Maybe I
can just climb
up after him," Ashlyn suggested.

"That's a good idea," Kirsty replied.
"But he'd probably just go higher."

"And we wouldn't want you to fall and
get hurt," Rachel added. "We've got to
come up with another plan."

She looked around the garden for a
ladder or another tool that she and
Kirsty could use, but there was nothing
around but flowers and more trees. Then
a beautiful monarch butterfly zipped by
and landed on Kirsty's arm.

"Look!" Rachel
pointed to her
friend's arm.

"Oh!" The
flower girls
gasped as they
gathered closer
to look at the

butterfly. They seemed to forget all
about the ribbon for a minute.

"It's so pretty," Tamara said softly. Her
sister nodded her head in agreement.

Rachel watched the butterfly softly

opening and closing its wings. If only she and Kirsty were tiny and had wings like the butterfly! Then they could zoom up into the treetops and get the ribbon back. Suddenly, she caught Kirsty's eye.

"Are you thinking what I'm thinking?" Kirsty asked her friend.

Rachel broke into a grin. "There's only one way to find out!"

Fabulous Photos

"Okay, girls," Kirsty told the flower girls. "It's your job to keep an eye on that gnome. Don't let him out of your sight! Rachel and I have to discuss something quickly. But we'll be right back."

Then she and Rachel stepped a few feet away.

"Psst!" Rachel whispered into the trees. "Blossom, we need you!"

The little fairy fluttered out from behind a tree.

"Do you have the ribbon?" she asked hopefully.

Kirsty shook her head and pointed to the goblin in the tree. He was busy throwing pinecones and making faces at the girls below him as he waved the ribbon tauntingly. But the girls weren't scared. They were collecting the pinecones in their flower-girl baskets, making pretty arrangements with the

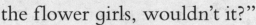

rose petals. And Talia and Tamara couldn't stop laughing at his silly faces.

"But we have an idea for getting it back," Kirsty explained quickly. "Can you turn us into fairies? Then we can fly up to the top of the tree and grab it."

Blossom shook her head.

"My magic powers are too weak right now," she said sadly. "And besides, it would be tough to explain that to the flower girls, wouldn't it?"

"I hadn't thought of that," Rachel said slowly, still trying to come up with a solution. Then she had an even better

idea. "What if we weren't the ones to fly up there?"

"What do you mean?" Kirsty asked, leaning forward eagerly to hear her friend's plan.

Rachel pointed to the spot on Kirsty's arm where the butterfly had landed just a few moments earlier.

"What if Blossom used just a tiny bit of her magic to ask a few butterflies to help us?"

"That's a great idea!" Kirsty agreed. Blossom nodded her head happily.

"Now *that*, I can do," she agreed with a smile.

With a small flick of Blossom's wand, a stream of sparkling flowers and butterflies appeared. The flowers hung

in the air for a second before they gently
popped and disappeared like bubbles.
But the butterflies fluttered closer to the
fairy. Kirsty and
Rachel watched with
delight as the fairy
whispered
to the
butterflies,
who then
flew off
into the
trees.

At first, nothing happened. But a
moment later, the butterflies returned
along with a few sparrows.

"There they are!" Blossom said,
fluttering her wings happily as the birds

and butterflies flew right up to the goblin. A bright orange monarch landed right on his nose.

"*Ah!*" the goblin yelled. "There's a bug on my face! Get it off! Get it off!"

He swatted at the butterfly, but it just darted away from him each time. Then two more butterflies joined in, landing on his ears.

"*Ooh, ohh!*" he shouted between giggles. "Get off me! That tickles. Stop it!"

Below him, the flower girls burst out laughing.

"It looks like those butterflies are tickling him," Ashlyn said as she covered her mouth with her hand.

The butterflies continued to create a distraction while the birds flew up to the treetop. One sparrow grabbed each end of the ribbon and quickly carried it back to Blossom. Before the flower girls even realized what had happened, Blossom grabbed the ribbon and darted out of sight.

Rachel and Kirsty knew it had shrunk back to fairy-size and was safe again.

"Thanks!" Blossom mouthed as she peeked out from behind a tree and dropped Talia's non-magical ribbon in front of Rachel and Kirsty. Rachel bent down to scoop it up before the flower girls noticed. Then she and Kirsty

watched as the fairy pointed her wand
at the girls and their damp, dirty dresses.
In the blink of an eye, the dresses were
dry, clean, and wrinkle-free. Blossom
waved to Rachel and Kirsty.

"Bye, girls!" she whispered. "I've got
to get back to Fairyland for the royal
wedding. But I'll see you soon. Keep a
close eye on my ribbon!"

Kirsty gave the fairy a quick wave before she disappeared with a flutter of her wings.

"Wow!" Avery marveled. "We're clean and dry again. Those garden gnomes really *are* magical!"

"And here's your ribbon back," Rachel said as she tied it around Talia's waist.

"Thanks!" The little girl said, bursting into a huge grin. Then she pointed to something behind them. "Look! It's the bride!"

Sure enough, Rachel and Kirsty turned to see Aunt Angela, the beautiful bride, and the rest of the wedding party hurrying toward them, followed by a flustered-looking photographer.

"So sorry to keep you all waiting," the photographer apologized with a shake of

his head. "Everything seemed to go wrong for me this morning. I just can't explain it."

Rachel elbowed Kirsty and glanced at her knowingly.

"Now that Blossom has her ribbon back, order and harmony has returned to weddings everywhere!" Rachel whispered happily to Kirsty.

Her friend nodded and smiled.

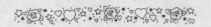

"Yup, looks like it!" she agreed.

"Let's take some photos!" Aunt Angela said with a brisk clap of her hands. "I'd like all the flower girls to stand here on this little bridge. But don't fall in!"

Kirsty, Rachel, and the girls laughed nervously. Aunt Angela had no idea what had happened when she had been gone, but no one was going to tell her now that everything was back on track.

The flower girls were on their best behavior as they took their places. As Avery reached up to fix her hair, her sister gasped.

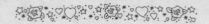

"Be careful!" Ashlyn said softly.
"There's a butterfly on top of your head!"

Sure enough, the girls quickly realized
that a butterfly had landed on each girl.
Some were perched on their baskets of
flowers, while others were on a shoulder
or in Avery's case—her head!

"They decided to stay for the photos!"
Mila said with a giggle.

Aunt Angela looked puzzled, but the bride was absolutely delighted.

"Those butterflies will look beautiful in the photos," she said happily. "What a perfect start to my wedding day."

Rachel and Kirsty couldn't have agreed more.

Flower Crown
Fiasco

Contents

The Missing Rings

After the photo shoot, Kirsty and Rachel helped lead the flower girls across the Botanical Garden to the rose garden, which is where the wedding ceremony was going to take place.

"These roses are so beautiful," Kirsty said with a sigh. "And they smell so

good, too. Isn't this a lovely place for a
wedding?"

Rachel took a deep breath, inhaling
the scent of the roses. Then she sneezed.

"Achoo!" Rachel rubbed her eyes.
"Well, I guess—if you don't have
allergies!"

Kirsty giggled. The
rose garden really
did look wonderful.
There was a small
stage set up
under an arbor
of flowers with
white folding
chairs arranged in a semicircle facing it.
Each chair had a perfect pink rose tied to
its back.

Aunt Angela was busy lining up the

bridal party at the back of the garden behind some moveable screens.

Meanwhile, the guests were beginning to arrive and take their seats. The flower girls lined up behind the ring bearer, a boy who was around six years old. His dad was the best man.

"When's this going to start?" Talia whined. "I'm hungry."

"Great!" Kirsty replied. "Because we have just the thing."

Luckily, she and Rachel had packed a bag just for this reason. Rachel reached into her backpack and pulled out a box of granola bars, which she distributed to the girls.

"Yum!" Avery said with a smile. "Thanks."

The girls were quiet as they ate their

snacks, which meant that Kirsty and Rachel could overhear the best man and his son talking.

"What do you mean, you left them at the hotel?" the man asked. He sounded angry.

"I thought you were going to bring the rings," the boy replied. "You told me I wasn't old enough. But we can go back to the hotel together to get them."

"We don't have time!" the father said impatiently. "The ceremony is about to begin. I thought I could trust you, but I guess I was wrong."

The little boy seemed very upset by his father's words.

"Uh-oh," Kirsty whispered to Rachel. "That doesn't sound good!"

Rachel nodded, her face serious. Her aunt and the best man were

busy talking now, and Rachel had a feeling it was about the rings.

"Oh, get it away from me!" one of the bridesmaids cried. It was the bride's sister,

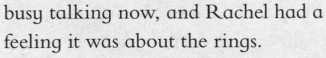

and she was shooing a giant fuzzy black-and-yellow bumblebee. But the bee continued to buzz around her head. The bridesmaid jumped backward to try to avoid the bee and ended up knocking the bride into a thorny rose bush.

"Ouch!" the bride cried as the thorns scraped her arm.

"Sorry," the bridesmaid replied. "Are you okay? That bee just wouldn't leave me alone."

"I'm fine," the bride snapped. "But you almost tore my dress—and ruined my wedding!"

The bride's sister looked hurt, and the bride still seemed very angry even though nothing terrible had actually happened to her or the dress.

"Kirsty," Rachel whispered. "I just had an awful thought. What if Jack Frost and his goblins got ahold of Blossom's flower crown?"

"Oh, Rachel, that would be terrible," Kirsty exclaimed. "But that would explain why everyone keeps snapping at people they love! The crown helps love stay strong in good times and bad."

As if to prove that something wasn't right, Talia leaned over and pinched her twin for no reason. Tamara burst into tears and rushed into the arms of one of

the bridesmaids, who also happened to be the girls' mother.

"Something's definitely wrong in Fairyland," Rachel groaned.

"But what can we do to help?" Kirsty asked.

"You girls can do me a huge favor!" Aunt Angela exclaimed as she suddenly appeared at Kirsty's side. "We need some new rings right away. The best man and the ring bearer left the real ones at the hotel, and there isn't enough time to go get them. So we need something else to use during the ceremony, or the wedding can't go on. You're both very

creative: Do you think you can find something in about twenty minutes?"

Rachel and Kirsty exchanged a glance.

"Sure, Aunt Angela," Rachel replied confidently. "You can count on us."

"Great," her aunt replied. "Thanks, girls. You're real lifesavers."

As soon as Aunt Angela was out of earshot, Rachel whispered her idea to Kirsty. They would have to use their magic lockets to get to Fairyland. There, they could help Blossom get her crown back while also searching for some stand-in rings. They knew that time would stand still in the human world while they were away.

Rachel and Kirsty dashed out of the rose garden and ducked behind some tall

lavender bushes. Then both girls grabbed the lockets they wore around the necks.

"One, two, three!" Kirsty said.

On three, the girls opened their lockets and sprinkled the glittery fairy dust over their heads. In just a few moments, they would be in Fairyland.

Wedding
Woes

The girls found themselves shrinking to fairy-size, surrounded by a cloud of glittery pink dust. They fluttered their wings gently as the sparkly fog cleared and they landed in front of Fairyland Palace.

There was obviously a big event happening—there were royal purple

flags and banners hanging from every
window and doorway, and there was a
long lavender carpet leading up to the
castle entrance.

Bertram the Frog greeted the girls at
the front door. He was wearing a fancy
black tuxedo.

"Good
afternoon, girls,"
Bertram said.
"You're here for the
royal wedding, yes?"
Rachel and Kirsty
glanced at each other.
Bertram thought they
were wedding guests!

"Well, not exactly," Kirsty replied.

"We're actually here to see Blossom the
Flower Girl Fairy," Rachel explained.

"We think she might need our help
with something, and we could use her
help, too!" Kirsty finished.

Bertram looked surprised.

"Well, Blossom is very busy today," he
explained. "But I'm sure she'll make time
to see both of you! I think I know just
where to find her. Follow me!"

Bertram hopped down a long
passageway, and the girls flew after him.
They ended up in an enormous banquet
hall, where the wedding reception was in
full swing. Some fairies were fluttering
around and dancing to the music while
other fairies nibbled on dainty, delicious-
looking appetizers.

"There she is!" Bertram announced.
He pointed to Blossom, who was
fluttering around a table with a giant

cake stand on it. Then Bertram waved
good-bye and hopped back toward the
castle's front door.

The girls noticed right away that there
was no cake on the stand. And Blossom
wasn't wearing her flower crown, either.
A second later, a beautiful fairy in a
shimmering white gown fluttered past
them, sobbing.

"Oh, it's just awful," she moaned.

Poor Blossom's wings drooped as she watched the distraught bride fly by. But when she saw Rachel and Kirsty she perked up a little.

"What a nice surprise!" Blossom exclaimed. "What are you two doing here?"

"We thought you might need our help," Rachel explained. "And we could use your help, too!"

Blossom hung her head.

"You're right," she said sadly. "Things aren't going well. Princess Rosalyn and Prince Arlo are having a terrible fight— and it's ruining their wedding day!

Princess Rosalyn forgot to order the wedding cake, and Prince Arlo is unhappy because there's no dessert for the guests. But I just know that cake or no cake, they wouldn't be fighting like this if I still had my flower crown."

Blossom touched her head as if to check to see if the crown had magically returned. Unfortunately, it hadn't.

"My crown helps control love in good times and bad, just like it says in the wedding vows. If I had my crown, Prince Arlo would realize the wedding cake isn't

as important as his new bride. But he's lost sight of what really matters."

"We thought that might have been what happened," Kirsty explained. "Everyone's been fighting at our wedding, too! In fact, the best man and ring bearer left the rings at the hotel and we have to find substitute rings."

"We thought your crown might be missing," Rachel added. "But if we can help you find it, we can save both weddings. Maybe we can retrace your steps to find it."

"That's a great idea," Blossom agreed. "I was definitely wearing it earlier today. I stopped by the dressing room on the third floor before the wedding. The bridal party was getting ready there, and I wanted to sprinkle the flower girl with some fairy dust to wish her good luck."

"To the dressing room, then!" Rachel cried. "We don't have a minute to lose!"

A Secret Portal

Kirsty, Rachel, and Blossom flew to the
third floor as quickly as they could.
The room was empty, but the bridal
party had left a lot of extra clothing
lying around. Rachel and Kirsty quickly
looked through all of the dresses, shirts,
sweaters, and shoes that the wedding

party had left behind. But the flower crown was nowhere to be found.

Kirsty had picked up a pretty pink sweater as she searched for the crown. She couldn't help holding the sweater up to herself and stealing a quick glimpse in the mirror.

"Kirsty!" Rachel scolded. "We don't have time for fashion. Wait— what was that?"

Rachel had caught a glimpse of something green moving in the mirror. She whirled around to look behind her friend.

"I think I just saw a goblin heading
down the hallway behind you!" Rachel
shouted. She, Kirsty, and Blossom
zoomed after the goblin. But the corridor
was empty.

"I was sure I saw something . . ." Rachel
mumbled as she glanced in the mirror a
second time. There it was again—a
goblin! Rachel looked behind her again,
but again, there was nothing there.

"I think I know what's going on,"
Blossom explained. "This must be a
magic mirror! There's one in the
Fairyland Palace and another in Jack
Frost's Ice Castle. The mirror is a secret
portal that leads from one place to the
other. The portal only opens when there's
a royal ball, though, and I guess the
wedding counts!"

"Wow," Kirsty murmured. "That's so cool."

"And I thought being a fairy was magical!" Rachel agreed. "Does that mean that goblin I saw is in Jack Frost's Ice Castle?"

Blossom nodded.

"And there's a good chance he took your flower crown, isn't there?" Kirsty asked.

"Yes," Blossom replied. "We should be able to follow him through the mirror. I just have to remember the spell my grandmother taught me when I was a

young fairy. It was so long ago, I need a minute to think of it."

Rachel and Kirsty waited as patiently as they could as Blossom muttered to herself, trying to recall the secret spell. Finally the fairy yelped happily.

"I've got it!" she said. Then she closed her eyes and recited the following:

"Magic mirror on the wall,

Today there is a fairy ball.

So open up your secret door,

And let fairies travel through once more."

Suddenly the center of the mirror began to spin, and a glowing ring of purple sparkles appeared.

"Let's go, girls!" Blossom called. "Fly straight through the ring of fairy dust!"

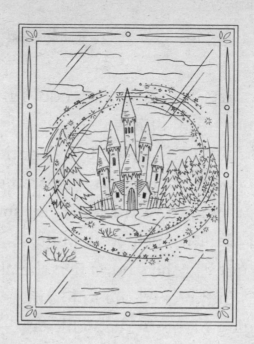

Kirsty and Rachel held hands and
followed Blossom through the mirror.

"Wow," Rachel said as they emerged
from the mirror inside Jack Frost's Ice
Castle. "That was amazing!"

"I know," Kirsty said, still in awe at
having flown through a magic mirror.
Fairyland was always full of surprises!
"Now how do we find the goblin who
stole your crown?"

"I'm not sure," Blossom admitted. "I've never been inside the Ice Castle before, so I don't know where to go."

Rachel thought about it for a minute. Where would the goblin be taking the flower crown?

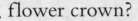

"I know!" Rachel cried. "We don't need to follow the goblin—we just have to find Jack Frost! The goblin will be bringing the crown to him."

"You're right," Kirsty agreed. "That's a great idea. But how do we know where Jack Frost is?"

As if in response, a chilly breeze wafted down the corridor to the right.

"Brrr," Blossom said, rubbing her arms to try to warm them up. "It's so cold here. I should have worn a sweater!"

"That's it!" Kirsty realized. "If we follow the cool breeze, it's sure to lead to Jack Frost."

They made a few turns and headed up a flight of stairs. The chilly air kept getting colder and colder until it felt as though they were inside a giant freezer. Finally,

they came to a room that was being
guarded by two goblins in suits of armor.

"Hide!" Blossom whispered quickly.
"Don't let the guards see you until we
have a plan."

Kirsty, Rachel, and Blossom ducked
behind a plant stand. The air was so
frigid the poor flower was frosted over.

"Jack Frost must be in that room,"

Rachel said. "Otherwise those guards wouldn't be standing there."

"But how are we going to get inside?" Kirsty asked. "We need that crown back or both weddings will be ruined!"

Cold as Ice

As Blossom and the girls tried to come up with a plan, the goblins began to argue.

"I can't wait until my shift is over," grumbled the first goblin.

"I know," moaned the second. "This armor is so uncomfortable."

"*Ugh!*" the first goblin agreed. "I have

an itch on my leg and I . . . just . . . can't scratch it."

He looked so silly wiggling around in the metal suit that Kirsty had to stifle a giggle. But the awkward suit had also given Kirsty an idea.

"The armor!" Kirsty whispered. "If the goblins can't see us, we can slip past them into the room." She leaned over and quickly explained her plan to Rachel and Blossom.

"Let's do it!" Blossom said. Then she, Rachel, and Kirsty flew out from behind the plant and darted way up and around the goblins. Luckily the pair of guards was so distracted they

hadn't even noticed. Rachel and Kirsty
hovered just above one of the goblin's
heads, where he couldn't see them. And
Blossom fluttered over the other goblin.

As planned, Blossom and the girls
pushed the eye covers on the metal suits
down so they slammed shut.

"Icky icicles!" one goblin exclaimed. "I
can't see!"

"Me, neither!" the other goblin cried as he stumbled into the first guard. With a crash, both goblins tumbled to the floor in a heap of clanking metal. Meanwhile, Blossom, Kirsty, and Rachel flew past them into the room they had been guarding. Sure enough, it was Jack Frost's throne room, complete with a giant icicle-covered chair in the center of the room.

Jack Frost was standing in a corner of the room in front of a

full-length mirror. He was wearing
Blossom's crown!

"Oh, look at me!" Jack Frost cackled.
"I'm an itty-bitty fairy. La-tee-da! I'm
so silly with my fluttery wings and my
sparkly fairy dust."

"Is that what you think I sound like?"
Blossom asked loudly, startling him.

Jack Frost whirled around, quickly
removing the crown.

"Fairies!" he shouted in surprise.
"W-what are you doing here? And how
did you get inside my castle?"

"The same way your goblins got inside
Fairyland Palace," Rachel explained.
"Through the magic mirror."

"Oh, drat!" Jack Frost muttered. Then
he pointed his wand at Blossom's crown.

"Cold and chilly is just as nice, freeze this crown until it's ice!"

"No, stop!" Blossom cried. "Don't freeze my crown. I need it back to save the royal wedding!"

"*Blech!*" Jack Frost spat. "Royal weddings are so boring. Who wants to go to a big, fancy party anyway?"

"Just because you didn't accept your invitation doesn't mean that others don't

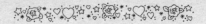

want to go," Blossom tried to reason with the grumpy troublemaker.

"Well, I might have gone if I'd been invited," Jack Frost grumbled, pouting. "But Queen Titania and King Oberon didn't send me an invitation."

"Really?" Rachel asked, puzzled.

"Yeah, it doesn't sound like the king and queen of the fairies to exclude anyone," Kirsty agreed.

Blossom flew over to a huge stack of unopened mail on a table in the corner of the throne room.

"Of course you were invited!" Blossom explained. "The king and queen actually considered taking your name off the guest list because the last time you attended a royal wedding, you almost ruined the party. But they wanted to

give you a second chance. Your
invitation is probably buried in this pile!"

Blossom waved her wand at the
unopened mail and a letter floated out
of the stack and into Blossom's hand.

"Here it is," Blossom said matter-of-
factly. Then she turned to Jack Frost and
gave him a stern look. "Maybe next time

you should read your mail! Now can I please have my crown back?"

"Of course not!" Jack Frost snapped, placing it back on his head. "Now that I have it, I want to keep it. I like it."

Blossom sighed. "I tried to ask nicely, but I guess we'll have to take back the crown, girls. On three . . . one, two, three!"

Blossom pointed her wand at the pile of mail, and a tornado of unopened letters swirled around the chilly villain.

"Ah, help!" Jack Frost cried. "I'm being attacked by mail!"

Rachel and Kirsty tried not to laugh as they swooped in and grabbed Blossom's crown off Jack Frost's head. It quickly shrank to fairy-size as they passed it back to Blossom.

"Thanks, girls!" Blossom cried happily as the letter tornado died down.

"No problem," Rachel replied. Then she flew down to pick up the piece of paper that had landed in front of her. She was curious: who had been sending Jack Frost so much mail? It was a letter from a publishing company.

"Dear Mr. Frost," she read aloud. "We regret to inform you that we are unable to publish your memoir, *Fantastic Jack Frost: The Story of My Life*."

Jack Frost crossed his arms grumpily and scowled at her.

"Go ahead, rub it in," he said. "But I'm not giving up. I'll be a famous author someday. And I'll be super rich!"

"Good luck with your book," Rachel told him. She turned to Kirsty. "Now that Blossom has her crown back, we really need to find rings for Aunt Angela's bride and groom!"

Happily Ever After

Blossom, Kirsty, and Rachel flew back
to the mirror as quickly as they could.
Blossom pointed her wand at the mirror
and recited the spell, and they flew through
the portal and back to Fairyland Palace.

"Let's go find the king and queen,"
Blossom suggested. "They'll know what
to do about the rings."

Back in the ballroom, Kirsty and Rachel were delighted to see that Princess Rosalyn and Prince Arlo were happily twirling above the dance floor.

"They're not arguing anymore!" Kirsty exclaimed, pointing to the happy couple.

"It's all thanks to you, girls," Blossom said with a smile. "Now that I have my crown back, their love will stay strong."

"And look!" Rachel cried. The Sugar and Spice Fairies had rolled a giant container of ice cream out onto the dance floor. They were busy scooping the treat into cups and handing them out to all the wedding guests. "It looks like someone figured out how to solve the dessert problem!"

At that moment, King Oberon and Queen Titania appeared.

"Thank you girls so much for your help," Queen Titania said. "You really saved the day."

"You're welcome," Rachel replied. "Now we're hoping the fairies can help us. We need to find something to use as wedding bands, and then we need to get back to our world."

King Oberon exchanged a glance with his wife. Then the king and queen slipped their own wedding rings off their fingers. Blossom waved her wand and— *poof!* A red satin box appeared. Blossom nestled the rings snugly in the box and handed it to Rachel.

"You can borrow these," King Oberon said. "Blossom will attend the wedding with you, and she'll bring them back after the ceremony. They've been sprinkled with fairy magic, too, so the rest of the wedding should be just perfect!"

"Thank you so much!" Kirsty said. "That's very generous! And even if it's not perfect, the wedding will turn out just fine because love will stay strong—in good times and bad."

The king and queen chuckled merrily
in agreement, then shooed the girls on
their way.

A moment later, Kirsty and Rachel
were behind the lavender tree at the
botanical garden. Their fairy wings were
gone, and they were human-size again.
Blossom landed on a tree branch next to
them and kicked up her feet.

"What a day!" she said with a sigh. "I'm going to take a rest here while you get those rings to your ceremony. I'll be right here when you're done. But take your time . . . and have fun!"

"Thanks!" Rachel said as she and Kirsty waved to the little fairy, who had nestled herself in beside the tree's leafy branches.

Then the girls dashed back to the rose garden to find Aunt Angela.

"There you are, girls," Aunt Angela greeted them with a relieved sigh.

"Here you go," Rachel said as she handed her aunt the red box, which had grown to human-size once the girls left Fairyland.

"Wherever did you get these?" Aunt Angela asked with a gasp. "They're beautiful!"

"Let's just say we had a little help from some friends," Kirsty replied, winking at Rachel. "These are just on loan until the best man gets the real rings from the hotel."

"Yes," Rachel chimed in. "We have to return these after the ceremony."

A few minutes later, the ceremony was ready to begin. Rachel and Kirsty took seats in the last row of chairs. A string quartet began to play the wedding march.

"Oh, look!" Kirsty cried. "Here come the flower girls."

She and Rachel watched proudly as the little girls marched down the aisle, sprinkling flower petals behind them, huge smiles on their faces. The bridesmaids and groomsmen followed. Then the music notes changed and the bride appeared.

"She looks so beautiful," Kirsty breathed as the bride walked down the aisle to meet the groom.

Rachel and Kirsty watched as the
couple exchanged their vows and slipped
the rings on to each other's fingers. As
soon as they did, a cloud of sparkling
butterflies burst from the flower arbor
over their heads, sending a shower of
glitter raining down on the happy
couple.

"I guess that's what King Oberon
meant when he said the rings had special

fairy magic on them," Rachel whispered
to Kirsty with a little laugh.

Based on their gasps and giggles, the
flower girls were delighted by the glitter.
And the bride was equally enchanted.

"What a magical surprise!" she said to
her husband, squeezing his arm happily.

The groom just smiled and leaned in to kiss his new wife.

"Fairy magic is fantastic!" Kirsty cried.

"It sure is," Rachel agreed. Now it was time for the reception, and she couldn't wait for the celebration to start!

RAINBOW magic™

Which Magical Fairies Have You Met?

- ☐ The Rainbow Fairies
- ☐ The Weather Fairies
- ☐ The Jewel Fairies
- ☐ The Pet Fairies
- ☐ The Dance Fairies
- ☐ The Music Fairies
- ☑ The Sports Fairies
- ☐ The Party Fairies
- ☐ The Ocean Fairies
- ☐ The Night Fairies
- ☐ The Magical Animal Fairies
- ☐ The Princess Fairies
- ☐ The Superstar Fairies
- ☑ The Fashion Fairies
- ☐ The Sugar & Spice Fairies
- ☐ The Earth Fairies
- ☐ The Magical Crafts Fairies
- ☑ The Baby Animal Rescue Fairies
- ☐ The Fairy Tale Fairies

■ SCHOLASTIC

Find all of your favorite fairy friends at
scholastic.com/rainbowmagic

HIT entertainment

RMFAIRY1

SPECIAL EDITION

Which Magical Fairies Have You Met?

- ☑ Joy the Summer Vacation Fairy
- ❏ Holly the Christmas Fairy
- ❏ Kylie the Carnival Fairy
- ❏ Stella the Star Fairy
- ❏ Shannon the Ocean Fairy
- ☑ Trixie the Halloween Fairy
- ❏ Gabriella the Snow Kingdom Fairy
- ☑ Juliet the Valentine Fairy
- ☑ Mia the Bridesmaid Fairy
- ❏ Flora the Dress-Up Fairy
- ❏ Paige the Christmas Play Fairy
- ❏ Emma the Easter Fairy
- ❏ Cara the Camp Fairy
- ❏ Destiny the Rock Star Fairy
- ❏ Belle the Birthday Fairy

- ❏ Olympia the Games Fairy
- ❏ Selena the Sleepover Fairy
- ❏ Cheryl the Christmas Tree Fairy
- ❏ Florence the Friendship Fairy
- ❏ Lindsay the Luck Fairy
- ☑ Brianna the Tooth Fairy
- ❏ Autumn the Falling Leaves Fairy
- ❏ Keira the Movie Star Fairy
- ❏ Addison the April Fool's Day Fairy
- ❏ Bailey the Babysitter Fairy
- ❏ Natalie the Christmas Stocking Fairy
- ❏ Lila and Myla the Twins Fairies
- ❏ Chelsea the Congratulations Fairy
- ❏ Carly the School Fairy
- ❏ Angelica the Angel Fairy
- ❏ Blossom the Flower Girl Fairy

3 stories in each one!

SCHOLASTIC

Find all of your favorite fairy friends at
scholastic.com/rainbowmagic

HIT entertainment

RMSPECIAL17

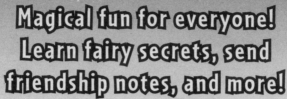

Magical fun for everyone! Learn fairy secrets, send friendship notes, and more!

SCHOLASTIC

HiT entertainment

www.scholastic.com/rainbowmagic

RMACTIV4